To Theodore

Remember i

in the butte

about (☺)

The Goosebump Goblin

D Bolen

Diane Banham

Book Three

The Dream Drifters Series

The Goosebump Goblin

Imagination can take you anywhere

Cover design by Leanne Brown at Sirenic Creations.
Dream Drifters image by Christy Ann at christyillustrates.com

For Will….

Trust me when I tell you just because you
cannot see it doesn't mean it isn't there.

CHAPTER 1

A Symphony from the Skies

Lightning smashed the cymbals, thunder battered on drums and driving rain beat like percussion pounding on the rooftops below. Reaching an almighty crescendo the storm announced its arrival like a symphony from the skies.

It surrounded Ember, Argent and Ammolite the three fearless dragons and their riders throwing them back and forth as they plunged into the cities house lined streets.

Nature had not created this weather of that Fitz was sure, it was something else, something evil that did not want to be found.

Had the lost Nightmare Pearl they were tracking sensed them?

Was this powerful storm a warning, a way of defending its prisoner and newfound freedom?

Fitz knew the answers to both, and it scared him deep inside.

"Stay on Bysidian and Templar's trail Ember, if we lose sight of their dragons now, we'll never find them again," he yelled using Noggin as a shield from the avalanche of hail. Even a dragon's fiery glow stood no chance against the elements this night.

"OUCH! That's it I officially hate Hail Hurlers," screamed Snitch buried behind Fitz as a large chunk of ice bounced off his fingers.

Noggin however did not make a sound. Laying her hand on Embers neck she was spellbound as the wind gathered strength and the swaying trees surrendered their leaves to the night.

Never had they had ridden in such a storm and the danger made her heart dance with exhilaration.

"Keep going, we're almost there," yelled Bysidian lowering himself into

Argent's neck as the dragon's wings skimmed the rain soaked roads.

"Hey, hold on a minute, what are those?" hollered Noggin snapping back to reality and wiping her water filled eyes.

Blurred by the slashing rain a pair of bright lights appeared in the distance and to Noggins horror she realised, they were heading straight towards them.

"Bysidian, Templar what are you doing, look in front of us don't you see them?" yelled Fitz pointing frantically.

"Stay with us Fitz just a little further, trust me," shouted Bysidian.

Faster and faster the beams grew larger as they closed in towards the dragons shining in their steely eyes. Black rubber tyres roared along the wet road and the glint of a silver radiator bearing down on them turned the approaching taxi from a machine into a monster.

"Almost there, a little more…."

"*WE'RE GOING TO DIE*," screeched Snitch as the heat of the engine swallowed him. Screwing up their eyes every muscle inside Noggin, Fitz and Snitch tensed bracing for impact.

"ARGENT NOW," Bysidian bellowed and in a flash his silver scaled companion shot from the taxis path leading the others from harm.

The vehicle careered past in a squall of spray and wind sending the dragons tumbling across the wet pavement and into a large glass canopied doorway.

"Am I dead, did it get us? " wailed Snitch as Embers talons screeched across the stone stopping herself seconds before they slammed into the doors.

"What was that a ridiculous game of Night Warrior chicken? Are you both trying to kill us?" snapped Fitz raising himself in his seat. Argent shook her waterlogged wing's showering him with spray as she and Bysidian hovered defiantly before them.

"Keep your anger and your opinions to yourself Fitz. We need to depend on each other down here and be a team. If you cannot do that and trust us, then you need to leave now."

THUD, THUD, THUD.

A loud knocking on the glass roof paused the boiling tension before Fitz could reply. Standing above them was a familiar ball of blue fluff waving like a lunatic and blowing a raspberry.

"Come down here and do that, I'll show you flaming Hail Hurlers," threatened Snitch waving a fist at the cheeky watcher.

With a howl of laughter and merry tap dance on the glass, the Hail Hurler vanished to join its friends in the foreboding skies above.

"That's it run away, when we get home, I'm going to find you and shave all that fluff off, let's see who's so cheeky then when you're bald and cold."

"Be quiet Snitch, look there's a sign, it might tell us where we are?" said Noggin pointing at large silver letters that shimmered in the lightning, "H-O-S-P…"

"Stop worrying Noggin Bysidian and I know exactly where we are, but we have to find somewhere to shelter from this weather and fast," interrupted Templar his saturated cloak draped limply on Ammolites green and orange scales.

Across the building, the tiny heroes flew battling the howling wind up over the rooftop when suddenly a weather ravaged garden appeared below.

"That's it, we must be able to find some shelter in there, follow me," said Templar.

Down they flew dodging the thrashing trees that littered the ground with branches and leaves but try as they might the dragons could not land.

"It's not safe there's too much debris," yelled Bysidian lifting an arm to deflect a stick twice the size of him.

A sudden flash of pink caught Noggin's eye.

"There look, that windows been left open we can get inside."

Desperate to rest the three dragons dodged the flapping curtain and flew in before collapsing on the windowsill. Noggin, Fitz and Snitch slid from Embers back and crumpled under their weary limbs.

"That was awesome," giggled Noggin sitting in a pool of water and picking bits of stick from her hair.

"Honestly Noggin you are so weird," said Fitz sliding off his dripping backpack and setting it down with a squelch.

"Ah, hello heat my friend I missed you," groaned Snitch as a welcome warmth drift across his wet skin from a radiator below. With a sharp shake of his head, Snitch freed the mass of white limp hair dripping down his neck making it stand back on end.

"I've said it once and I'll say it again, I don't like those sneaky Hail Hurlers and come to think of it, Wind Woozels are not top of my favourite list right now either."

The radiator called to the dragons, it was the perfect place to recharge their tired bodies for the flight home so leaving their riders to dry all three hopped down and nestled between the pipes to warm their cold hard scales.

"Ammolite no falling asleep in there, do you hear me?" ordered Templar pulling off a long black boot and pouring out a stream of icy water.

Noggin and Fitz dangled their legs above the radiator making water drops fizzle and hiss as they fell from their shivering feet onto the hot metal.

"*Ugh*, what is that vile smell it's disgusting?" cried Noggin grasping her red runny nose.

"Ember was that you?"

Snitch dropped his sodden boots next to her and stretched his green stripy socked toes out into the stream of warm air.

"Oh Snitch put them back on it smells like something died in those socks."

"I'll have you know I put these on clean this morning with my weekly change of underpants… or was it

18

yesterday … or it could have even been the day before… oh who cares Noggin?"

"For once will you two give it a rest," interrupted Fitz, "we have more important things to do here than worry about Snitch's feet though I do agree with Noggin, they stink Snitch. Are you sure this is the right place?" he asked turning to Bysidian.

Nodding slowly Bysidian gazed into the dark room, "It's here exactly where The High Minster said it would be, I can feel it."

"Who's there? Who are you?"
A voice from the shadows called.

CHAPTER 2

Singeing Snitch Hair

"Did you hear that?" whispered Snitch. "Someone else can hear us but how? Have I missed something did we land in a child's nightmare because I thought we were only here to scoop up that lost black ball of trouble and high tail it out of town?"

"That was the plan," replied Fitz as confused as his teammate.

Blinking hard to focus their tired eyes four identical beds gradually appeared in the dim light, two on either side of the room and each with a long curtain hanging by the side.

"Oh, of course, a hospital that's what the sign said," whispered Noggin.

"Well, that explains the funny smell," said Snitch scrunching up his nose.

"What clean?" asked Noggin. "Forgive me I forgot you don't know what that is."

Keeping as still as possible the tiny visitors began to look for the source of the mysterious voice.

"Snitch are your gloves dry yet?" whispered Templar, "we could do with some help here."

21

"I'm not sure that's a good idea," replied Snitch, "I'll give them a try, but I warn you if they work, they'll light up the room. Whoever is out there will be able to see us as well as hear us."

"They already know we're here Snitch, it makes no difference if they see us, do it."

Slowly he lifted his hands and clapped. *POP!* "*Ow wow wow that hurt,*" squealed Snitch as a purple spark flew along his arms and faint wisps of lilac smoke drifted from his hair ends.

Noggin giggled, "Lovely, singeing Snitch hair, well at least that got rid of your funny clean smell."

"Try again," ordered Bysidian
impatiently.

'Really? Would you like to try?"
snapped back Snitch shaking his tingling
pins and needles hands.

The look on Bysidian's face answered
that question, it was the look only
Snitch's mother gave him when he was in
humongous trouble usually for answering
back.

Closing his eyes Snitch drew back his
hands and braced himself for pain.

CLAP... with a crackle and soggy fizz
the gloves sparked into life along with his
Seeker glasses lighting up his frightened
face for all to see.

Sputter-pop-pop… Snitch quickly scanned the room before the wet glasses cut out.

"I see four children, all sound asleep so no one should be able to see or hear us. I don't see any… no wait the far bed… darn it." With one last *POP!* the glasses died.

"Please don't hurt us, we didn't do anything, we didn't tell anyone I promise," pleaded the sobbing voice.

Noggin looked at Fitz and the others. Whoever that was they were scared, they needed help and she was unwilling to sit there and not do anything.

Edging forward Noggin lowered herself from the windowsill until she dangled above the radiator.

"Be careful," instructed Bysidian as she dropped onto Embers back being mindful to avoid the hot metal. "It could be a trick, that pearl knows we are coming I'm sure of it."

"Bysidian I've heard enough children cry in their nightmares to know when something is a trick," she replied. "It breaks my heart to hear them, I have to help whoever that is."

Flying free of her warm resting place Ember glided quietly across the room. Snitch was correct all four children were fast asleep, but they were not enjoying happy dreams.

"Try the far bed Noggin I saw something there," called Snitch.

Landing softly Noggin cautiously approached a sleeping girl, her beautiful long blonde hair lay tousled on her pillow wet from the fat tears rolling down her cheeks.

"She's crying Ember but it's not her calling so who is?"

Noggin stopped and listened, the sobbing was now mixed with loud sniffs and they appeared to be coming from below her feet. Following the sound, Noggin climbed down the untucked bedsheets and looked beneath the bedframe.

"Oh my," she gasped.

Huddled in the furthest corner, her knees pulled in tight to her chest and large eyes staring wide with terror was a girl in her pyjamas and fluffy dressing gown.

"It's alright I'm not going to hurt you, please don't cry," reassured Noggin dangling from the sheet. "What are you doing under there?"

"Hiding," whispered the girl, "we all are."

"*All?*" asked Noggin dropping to the floor.

Slowly the shaking girl lifted her arm and pointed to the bed across from hers just as a small bare foot disappeared underneath. Below the third bed, a bandaged face appeared listening to their voices and from the movement, under the fourth, someone was hiding there too.

"Guys you had better get over here, something strange is happening," called a confused Noggin to the windowsill watchers.

Having dried out Fitz and Snitch hopped aboard a dragon each and flew towards Noggin.

"No please don't wait for us you two, help yourself to our dragons no problem at all," said Templar sarcastically as he and Bysidian jumped to the floor landing with a crunch.

Lifting his boot Bysidian pulled out a small black shard stuck in the worn tread.

"That's not good boss," said Templar glancing at his leader.

Bysidian shook his head, "it's loose in here somewhere, stay alert my friend," and they ran to join the others.

CHAPTER 3

The Goosebump Goblin

"Are they real dragons?" asked the frightened girl who introduced herself as Chloe. She seemed reluctant to show her face and instead hid part of it with her dressing gown hood and long hair.

"Sure are but don't worry they're friendly," assured Fitz as Chloe tentatively stretched out a fingertip and stroked Embers back.

"Wow, you're so toasty."

Suddenly the bed above began to move violently, bouncing and shaking like an earthquake. Chloe lowered her head as the mattress dipped and the frame creaked then as fast as it started it stopped.

"What was that?" asked Snitch swiftly letting go of the armour clad arm he'd grabbed in fright much to Templar's disgust.

"That was just me turning over in my sleep from the bad dreams."

"What bad dreams Chloe?" asked Fitz before he stopped, "hold on, that's you up there asleep in the bed?"

"Yep, that's me, just like the others in here Max, Luke and Lottie. We try so hard not to fall asleep because when we do, it comes." Chloe's voice trembled in fear.

"What comes?" asked Noggin moving closer making Chloe pull her hood further across her face.

"We call it the Goosebump Goblin. None of us understands it but we fall asleep and the next thing we know is we're hiding under our beds with no idea how we got here. Even stranger at the same time we are still fast asleep above. Down here's the safest place to be believe me."

"The Goosebump Goblin," uttered Snitch in terror as real goosebumps sprang to attention along his arms. "I don't like the sound of that one little bit."

"Are you telling me that thing is out of the pearl and running around?" demanded Noggin looking at the Night Warriors.

"This Goosebump Goblin, when did it appear exactly?" asked Bysidian ignoring Noggins glare.

"Erm, about 3 days ago. Max brought in that tiny black ball he found in the gardens after a visit from his parents and it appeared that night."

"I didn't mean to drop it," huffed Max scurrying under the bed to join them. "It slipped as I went to show Luke over there and smashed," he said pointing to the bed next door. "Boring nurse doesn't like us bringing in things from outside as they could bring in germs so I scooted the pieces under the radiator and down the pipe holes in the floor so she wouldn't see."

"*SHUSH*, it's coming," hushed a second girl's voice from across the room.

"Keep quiet Lottie, it'll be ok," reassured a boys voice, presumably Luke who was hiding below the bed next door.

Peeping below the bedsheets they watched and listened.

From the quiet corridor outside the sound of bare feet slapping on the hard ground grew louder as it approached.

An ominous shadow appeared through the ward door cast like a spindly giant across the floor until it reached the window beyond. Max and Chloe gulped as they watched the shadow through eyes wide with fear.

Abruptly the footsteps stopped as a pair of large dirty and extremely knobbly feet appear. They had scruffy yellow chipped toenails and were covered with bristles of thick black hair rising to a pair of pale thin boney ankles and scrawny hairy legs.

The feet took one step into the room before stopping again. First, they turned left and then right before spinning around and leaving in haste. The shadow followed leaving the children to breathe a heavy sigh of relief.

"The goblin never stays in here," whispered Max, "we don't know why but it doesn't seem to like it."

Before he could finish Bysidian and Templar bolted from beneath the bed and to the door watching the unwanted visitor as it vanished into the ward next door.

"It can't be," gasped Bysidian looking at Templar with disbelief before sprinting after it.

"Hey, hold on wait for us," called Fitz as his team followed leaving four confused children and the dragons to slip back to the warmth of the radiator pipes.

Hugging the wall five tiny figures ran along the bright corridor until they reached next door. With a silencing finger on his lips, Bysidian led the way into the room edging around the door frame and whizzing under the nearest bed.

As the rain hammered against the windowpane they hid and watched between the bursts of lightning.

The curious creatures' feet moved swiftly between the beds as if searching for something in particular. No children were hiding below these beds, everyone appeared to be sleeping soundly.

With a grunt, the feet unexpectedly disappeared as the creature jumped onto a bed it had selected.

Moving to get a better view the tiny watchers gazed in astonishment at the sight that greeted them.

The Goosebump Goblin was a small creature with big feet and skinny legs. Dressed in a pair of tattered patched trousers ripped off at the knee its only other clothing was a battered leather waistcoat and a roughly stitched bag slung over one shoulder.

Long thin arms gave way to huge hands that swung by its side and poking from beneath its scruffy matted black hair were a pair of long pointed ears.

Skilfully the Goosebump Goblin stepped over a sleeping girl until it came to rest staring at her face so close, it could feel the child's warm breath on its pasty white skin.

Gently placing one long finger on the tip of her nose the goblin closed its black eyes.

"What's it doing?" whispered Snitch in horror.

"Shush blabbermouth," hissed Noggin slapping her hand across Snitch's mouth. "Do you want it to hear us?"

A faint blue glow appeared deep inside the girl's nose, brighter and brighter it started at the bridge between her eyes and moved down until it oozed out of her nostril. The goblin's eyes lit up as it delicately hooked the bright bead of light with a dirty pointed fingernail. Admiring the glow for a moment it paused then holding an old sock beneath let it drop inside before stuffing the sock into the bag.

The goblin then began to rummage around inside its scruffy trouser pocket and eventually pulled out a clenched fist covered in blue dust. Taking a deep breath, it blew a cloud of pale blue into the innocent child's face then stood back and watched.

It only took a moment for the girl's eyes to begin to flicker, and her arms twitched as she cried out in her slumber. This seemed to please the creature as it clapped its hands in delight sending clouds of blue powder into the air.

"What is that thing and what's it doing?" whispered Fitz, "I've never seen a nightmare like that before."

"That's no ordinary nightmare Fitz it's a Snacchen," whispered Bysidian not taking his eyes off the creature. "I didn't think I would ever see one in my time as a warrior, they are rarely seen and incredibly powerful."

With a snigger, the creature patted the girl tenderly on her flushed pink cheek then hopped from the bed and ran from the room with its precious sock treasure.

"What was that thing, what's a Snacchen?" asked Noggin as they ran back to the children hiding in the ward.

"Bad news, that's what a Snacchen is, I cannot believe there was one in the vault all that time and we didn't know," said Templar.

"The last time I knew of one was when I started training to become a Night Warrior. They are so dangerous none of us was allowed into the Nightmare Vault when Solomon entered the pearl to …" Bysidian's voice faded. "He didn't destroy it, Solomon knew it was still alive in there all this time. He must have hidden the pearl knowing he would return for it one day.

A Snacchen Noggin is not simply a thing from a child's imagination, it's the nightmare before all nightmares and evil to the core."

CHAPTER 4

Hopes and Wishes

"It's alright you can come out it's gone," announced Noggin.

Slowly the children crept from beneath their beds and as they did the corridor light caught Chloe's face revealing a large scar covering most of the left side.

"It's alright you can stare, everyone else does," she sighed noticing Snitch looking at her before turning his glance away in embarrassment. "I'm ugly I

44

know. The mean kids at school remind me all the time and grownups stare everywhere I go. The doctors say another operation should help but I'm not so sure."

"Oh no Chloe please don't say that, you're not ugly I think you are beautifully unique and extremely brave," said Noggin. "There is only one of you in this whole wide world and that is your superpower, you're a hero Chloe always remember that."

Max had a large bandage wound around his head and a cast over most of his left arm.

"What happened to you?" asked Fitz.

"I decided it would be cool to see how fast I could ride my skateboard off my dad's shed roof," said Max. "Took me ages to get the ladder up there as well but it didn't quite go to plan."

"You don't say," said Luke dragging himself from under his bed as Max hurried to help with his one good arm. "Being an idiot is your superpower isn't it Max?"

"Ignore Luke he doesn't mean it, he's just frustrated with his leg and angry at the kid that did it. He doesn't understand it was an accident," whispered Chloe.

Luke had a frame around his lower right leg. Large metal rings held together by pins and wires that disappeared into his skin.

"Football accident," he said sliding painfully towards the curious faces. "Some stupid kid tackled me and snapped my bone clean through in two places. The doctor calls it a complex fracture whatever that is. Now I can't use my leg until it heals and that will be a while. No more footie for me," he said with tears welling in his eyes he tried unsuccessfully to hide.

"Remarkable," said Snitch examining the frame, "well I think it looks amazing, like a robot or something from space but whatever happens don't let Miss Gadgets here near it she will have it stripped into pieces before you can blink."

"What's wrong with wanting to know how things work, how else am I supposed to learn Mr Tech Head?" replied Noggin.

Luke began to look a little worried he didn't like the idea of Noggin touching his frame never mind disassembling it.

"Ignore him Luke I am not going to touch your leg I promise, but I would like a closer look at some point the Guardians back home would be fascinated."

"Oh Lottie I'm so sorry are you alright under there?" asked Chloe lifting Lottie's bed covers whilst being careful not to wake the sleeping Lottie above.

"I'm fine don't worry about me?" replied Lottie taking Chloe's hand and carefully sliding from under her bed. Across both eyes, she had a large padded bandage.

"Lottie just had an operation on her eyes," whispered Max to Fitz and the others, "they have told her that she may never see again."

"Never is a strong word Max, things just take some time that's all, give Lottie's eyes a chance," replied Fitz.

"What I don't understand is how come you guys are all here under the beds yet still asleep on top of them?" said a puzzled Noggin.

Fitz had been thinking the same and had a theory, "I think it's because this is where the pearl smashed, and that creature escaped. We're inside the children's nightmares as usual, but all of them are having the same one which is a little odd. They are asleep in bed but awake in the nightmare, and hence we're here together."

"Yes, yes, I get that," interrupted Snitch impatiently, "but what was that thing and what did it pull from that poor girl's nose? Was it her brain?" Snitch began to melt into a panic like only he could, "it's a brain munching snot picking goblin, *we're all doomed*."

"Oh Snitch don't be so dramatic," huffed Noggin before glancing sideways to Bysidian for a shake of his head to confirm it wasn't her brain.

"A Snacchen…."

"Goosebump Goblin," interrupted Noggin bossily. "It gives me goosebumps and it is certainly a goblin, so I have officially renamed it. Snitch put it in the Guardians library right now."

Bysidian ignored her and continued, "…is an incredibly powerful creature and almost impossible to catch. They can travel through anything reflective, like mirrors, glass or water and are lightning fast." As if on cue a flash filled the sky outside making everyone jump.

"Yes, yes it does that, we saw it leap into the big glass doors at the end of the corridor and it didn't come out the other side, it just vanished into thin air," said Chloe.

"Where they go, nobody knows as no one has ever managed to follow one. They steal children's hope and wishes, their dreams for the future that was the bright light it took from the girl's nose," said Bysidian.

"So let me get this right, the Goosebump Goblin is actually called a Snacchen and they pull things from our noses that are not our brains?" asked Luke as the others nodded. "It came from inside that black ball Max found in the gardens and now it's loose in the hospital because clumsy *Max* dropped it. Those are real dragons, and you are tiny people trying to catch it?"

"Yep, that's about it, sounds crazy I know," said Snitch clapping his gloves together producing his keyboard.

"Wow, how did you do that?" asked Max in astonishment, anything techy or dangerous captivated him.

"With a little bit of Snitchy Magic," replied Snitch proudly as his glasses began to sparkle and fill with information from the Guardians library.

"Snitchy magic, oh please when did you come up with that one?" sniggered Noggin.

Snitch did what he did best and ignored Noggins rudeness.

"Here we are Snacchen's. There doesn't seem to be anything more than Bysidian has already told us, and certainly nothing on how to catch one. It seems there are lots of them, but they are rarely seen so no one knows much about them."

Continuing to read further Snitch suddenly stopped.

"Wait a moment," his voice drifted away. Bysidian discreetly shook his head in warning as Snitch's wide magnified eyes moved to his.

"What is it Snitch, what did you see?" asked Noggin but her teammate did not answer and hastily clapped his hands to close the files.

"Why doesn't it stay in here, it goes in all the other wards?" asked Chloe rescuing Snitch from a reply.

"It must be the pearl pieces Max hid," said Fitz, "it can feel them, and it has been locked up in that prison for so long it's scared of going back. Understandable I suppose."

"That thing doesn't look like it's scared of anything to me," said Max with a shudder.

"Everyone's scared of something Max, just some are better at hiding it than others," said Noggin. "Take Snitch here, he's afraid of anything and everything and boy does he show it. If a butterfly farted, he'd be running for the hills."

The children giggled as Snitch raised his hand.

"And I'm not afraid to admit it, there is nothing wrong with being scared," he confessed.

The sound of running feet was upon them before they realised. With no time to get back under the beds, they all froze in fear.

The Goosebump Goblin ran straight past the open door without a glance inside and hanging from his bag were several odd used socks all glowing brightly.

"Hey, you that's my sock," cried Max causing the footsteps to stop for a moment before speeding away. "That thing stole my sock, Mum has been looking for that everywhere. No wonder I have so many odd pairs in my bag. Does it know how much trouble I'm in for losing them?"

"Ooh the Goosebump Goblin is the Sock Monster," said Lottie. "I knew it existed and it wasn't the washing machine eating them all."

"Oh yes Lottie the Sock Monster exists, we've met a few times but to be fair he's a nice guy who just likes to keep his 752 feet warm, certainly not like that goblin," said Templar.

"What does it do with them all?" asked Max curiously. "Why does it want the hopes and wishes that belong to other people, surely they are of no use."

"Well they must be of some use," added Snitch "or why would it want them? Maybe it eats them."

"What along with the brains nincompoop, now stop it you're scaring everyone," snapped Noggin looking at the four terrified children's faces.

"So how do we catch it?" asked Luke with a deep breath. "If you came to capture it you must have a plan, right?"

"There may be a slight snag with that Luke, you see we didn't know exactly what was inside that particular Nightmare

Pearl until we got here," replied Noggin. "So right now the plan is evolving shall we say."

"Which in Noggin language means we are making it up as we go along," added Snitch.

"Okay fair enough you didn't know what was inside but how did it get here and where did it come from, in fact, where did you all come from?" asked Max.

"Wow, now that's a *long* story," said Fitz.

"Well, you'd better start talking fast before it comes back then hadn't you."

CHAPTER 5

Bogies in Butter

"Pirates, that's so cool," said Max excited to hear they actually existed and not just in stories.

"No not cool at all, it's very uncool," said Snitch with a shiver. "They are evil and have no cares whatsoever about unleashing these nightmares on anyone."

"I wish I could meet the Frost Fairies and Ice Imps," said Chloe they sound wonderful but I'm not so sure about Squidgeable slugs. They may be a bit slimy for me."

"No, I would take the Hail Hurlers and bouncing beetles over girlie fairies and imps any day," said Luke. "They sound like loads of fun and trouble rolled into one, a bit like me."

"Well, I would like to meet the Kissing Granny," said Lottie "she just sounds like she wants a bit of love and cuddles."

"Have you lost your mind?" said Snitch, "she would suck your face off and make you eat boiled sweets all day until your teeth fell out. Don't let that wrinkly exterior fool you."

The sound of running feet appeared again, and a door swung back and forth as the Goosebump Goblin continued with its work when suddenly another pair of footsteps approached this time wearing shoes.

"A nurse is coming quick hide," said Chloe as they darted under the nearest bed leaving poor Luke stranded in the middle of the floor trying in a desperate panic to pull himself undercover.

Too late, the nurse walked into the ward and Luke froze, closing his eyes he held his breath, he was going to have a lot of explaining to do.

The footsteps came closer and closer until they were almost on top of him but to his astonishment, the nurse walked right by. Confused Luke opened his eyes slowly and watched as the nurse did his rounds, checking on each of the sleeping children before he straightened Lottie's bed covers.

"I don't know what you guys dream about, but it sure makes a mess of your covers every night, " he whispered as he tucked each sleeping child in. His rounds done the nurse turned and headed for the door missing Luke's hand with his foot by a whisker.

"Did you see that?" cried Noggin as silence fell back in the room and the others crept from their hiding places.

"He didn't see me, it was like I was invisible," said Luke in shock.

"Now this is getting very freaky indeed," muttered Max rubbing his head bandage. "Why didn't he see you, he almost trod on you."

"He did see you, look safely asleep in your bed," explained Fitz pointing to the sleeping Luke. "He can't see you in the nightmare we're inside, that's all in your minds."

"Oh, brain ache," groaned Snitch.

"Hold on so if the nightmare children are invisible to the nurses, does that mean the goblin is as well?" asked Noggin.

"I think so yes."

With that, an even more confused Snitch buried his face in his hands.

"No time to worry about that," said Bysidian taking charge, "we need to find that goblin and fast before it steals every hope, wish and dream from every poor child in here."

A loud bang and clatter echoed down the corridor from somewhere out of view.

"That'll be the goblin, it likes chocolate and sugary things," said Chloe. "It pinched my chocolate bar from beside my bed last night and it has discovered the vending machine along the hall. It's been trying to get into it ever since."

"Yeah, Chloe and I have been watching it the last few nights, it's crafty," said

Max. "It has been all over the place including the staff canteen where it picked huge lumps of yellow wax from its ears and dropped them into the milk in the fridge."

"Please tell me you took the milk away when it had gone?" asked Fitz. This question was followed by a pause, "I'll take that as a no then," he groaned looking at the two cheeky grins.

"You think that's bad, you should see what it does with its bogies and the butter," whispered Chloe.

"At least you two get to watch that thing," huffed Luke. "Lottie and I have to stay here, I'm useless with my smashed leg and Lottie can't see."

"Yes, we want to help," said Lottie, "there must be something we can do?"

BANG, BANG, BANG

The goblin was getting frustrated with the machine and the precious goodies locked beyond its reach. As the storm outside grew stronger the frustrated bangs were drowned out by an ear splitting roll of thunder.

"Great more thunder, I hate thunder and lightning," wailed Chloe touching her face. Chloe's burn had happened from a firework accident and anything hot or loud terrified her.

"Oh I love it, I love watching storms, all the colours and swirling clouds but of course ..." said Lottie as her voice faded away from the realisation, she may never see one again. "I wish I could see then I could help you."

"Yeah well, I wish I could walk then I wouldn't be stuck here, useless," snapped Luke crossly. "In my dreams," he mumbled.

"Of course that's it," cried Fitz loudly. Pulling his backpack off he reached inside and pulled out a golden Dream Pearl laying it carefully on the floor.

"What is that?" asked Max as it shone across the staring faces making them shimmer with rainbows.

"A Dream Pearl," explained Noggin. "Inside is a wonderful dream created by the Guardians, it must be for one of you guys."

"If you had a dream, right now Luke what would it be?" asked Fitz.

"That's easy, to get this stupid thing off my leg and to be able to walk and play football," said Luke without hesitation.

"Do you truly think this will work?" asked Snitch looking at Fitz with worry across his face.

"I have no idea, I've never opened one inside a nightmare before never mind whilst the nightmare is still loose, but it has got to be worth a shot, hasn't it?"

"Do it," ordered Bysidian, "we are going to need all the help we can get to catch that thing."

With a gentle hand, Chloe placed Fitz on Luke's bed. Carefully he carried the golden pearl across sleeping Luke before clambering under his pillow. Resurfacing a moment later with his black hair ruffled Fitz stood back and waited.

"Anything happening?" called Snitch as everyone looked on patiently.

"Well he's stopped squirming around so much and it looks like he's smiling, so something is, but I'm not sure what."

"*MY LEG*," cried Luke sat on the floor, "*LOOK*."

Bit by bit the metal frame around Luke's leg began to fade until it vanished completely. His once broken leg was straight with not a single mark, it was as if nothing had ever happened."

"Careful, take it easy," said Noggin as Luke rolled down his pyjama leg and tried to stand. Wobbly at first, he held onto a bed frame and steadied himself until he stood proudly for everyone to see.

"I can stand, and walk," he whispered taking a few steps with tears in his eyes.

"A dream within a nightmare, well I never," said Templar with a smile.

"CHOCOLATE IS MINE," screeched a voice as the battered machine finally gave in and dropped a bar to the goblins delight.

"Please could someone tell me what is happening," asked Lottie in frustration.

"Luke said he is standing up, but I don't understand how that's possible,"

"How would you like to see for yourself Lottie?" asked Fitz taking a second pearl from his bag.

"Another one," said Noggin in surprise.

"Oh, more than two Noggin I have four in here. The Guardians insisted I bring them all and I wondered why but now I understand."

Crawling from beneath sleeping Lottie's pillow Fitz and the others waited. "My eyes are tingling," said Lottie placing her hands across them. "Boy they feel strange, Chloe are you there, can you help me please?"

Chloe reached behind her head to undo the tape and unwind the bandages. Lottie sat with her eyes closed as her hands began to tremble.

"Open your eyes," said Chloe calmly.

"I can't, I'm scared."

Noggin took hold of Lottie's little finger and squeezed it gently.

"What colour are your eyes?"

"Green," whispered Lottie. "My mum says they are as green as the finest emeralds in the world."

"Like mine and Embers, we each have green eyes. If you open yours, you will see."

Slowly Lottie's eyelids opened, just a slit at first before opening wide.

"Everything's a bit blurry," she said blinking a few times before the widest smile spread across her face. Noggin ran to stand in front of her and waved.

"Hi Noggin," said Lottie giggling at the little person as she became crystal clear. Grabbing Chloe's hand Lottie smiled at the unseen face of her friend.

"Me next," begged Chloe as Fitz left a pearl below her sleeping head. With her scar gone and her cheek as smooth as the other Fitz crawled under Max's pillow and left his last Dream Pearl.

"Surely something should have happened by now?" asked Bysidian as Max sat on the ward floor still in his cast and bandage with everyone staring at him.

74

An odd sound came from outside the room, a sort of rumbling rolling sound coming closer.

"What on earth is that?" asked Snitch as Noggin ran to the doorway and peeped out.

"YAHOOO!!!"

The Goosebump Goblin whizzed past with chocolate smeared around its face riding a shiny new skateboard painted in red and yellow flames. Reaching a bend in the corridor Noggin watched as the goblin crashed headfirst into the wall and in a flurry of wrappers ran from sight.

Everyone turned towards Max who had turned his eyes to the ceiling, so he didn't have to acknowledge their stares.

"Nice ride Max," said Noggin biting her bottom lip and smirking at Bysidian's disgusted face.

"What? I needed a new skateboard and besides I have one good arm, I can still help."

"We should move before it comes back," said Bysidian, "the Snatc... sorry Goosebump Goblin may not like it in here, but don't forget it can still see us."

"Oh, I see *yooou*, I see *yoooOOu*," came the eerie voice singing the words from out of sight.

"Quick under here," said Luke as they piled under his bed and dragged the covers down to hide.

76

Outside the thunder rolled and with a flash of lightning, the covers flew up as the goblins face appeared. Lottie squealed in fright, she had never seen the evil creature before and here it was face to face with her.

"I see you good, I know you are here. I smell nice dreams and Guardians pearls. You think you hide from me, well I know," as it grinned showing a mouth full of mouldy teeth.

Bysidian and Templar rushed forward swords drawn.

"You do not belong here," yelled Templar over the thunder. "You're coming with us and if you resist, we will have to banish you right here and now."

The goblin howled with laughter, "I think not puny Night Warriors."

Its laughter suddenly stopped, and two pure evil black eyes glared at Bysidian and Templar.

"He promised me I would be set free, and instead he abandoned me in that pearl prison hell locked inside your stupid vault. *He* lied and *you* have to pay for that."

"Move aside," yelled Fitz as he ran forward a Dream Catcher pearl in hand ready to pull it open.

"*Never*, I am *never* going back inside one of those," screeched the goblin as it threw down the covers and bounced across the beds. With an almighty leap, it hurtled through the window glass and made its escape.

"Look it dropped a sock," cried Max running across the room and picking up the glowing fluffy sock on the floor.

Pulling open the top Max's face was instantly alight with blue as the hopes and wishes trapped inside softly called to him.

"Listen, they need our help," he said reaching in and carefully pulling out the glowing bead. "What can we do, how do we help you?" he asked the voices as he cupped them in his palm.

Deep within the cold light, Max could see a ballet dancer, dressed in a crystal encrusted white tutu with pale pink silk slippers.

Dancing to beautiful music she twirled in a magnificent theatre full of people watching. As she finished the applause rang out and the audience rose to their feet breathless from her performance.

Max beamed from ear to ear transfixed by the dancer and the dream unfolding before him, he felt as if he were right there sharing in her happiness.

"NO, NO somethings wrong," Max shrieked as the light grew dull and the calling voices quietened.

"It's dying someone please help me," he cried in desperation to the others as the dim light flickered one last time then went out leaving in his hand only a sprinkling of blue dust.

Dashing to poor Max's side everyone watched as the dust drifted away in the draft from the open window.

"They died, that girls hope and wishes died when Max took it from the sock, why?" asked Lottie almost crying.

"They don't belong to Max," said Snitch with sadness on his face. "They were another child's hope and wishes not Max's so when he touched them, they died."

"She wanted to be a ballet dancer," sighed Max his voice quivering with sadness.

"We have to stop that thing," snapped Templar clambering up Lottie's dressing gown and jumping to the windowsill.

Pushing on the glass he tried to see where the goblin had gone.

Lottie pulled in the curtain and closed the window whilst the rain streamed down the glass as if the sky were crying with her.

"THERE HE IS," she exclaimed as the Goosebump Goblin danced past a window in the building opposite and gave them a toothy grin followed by a rude finger gesture.

"Snitch we're going to need a map of this place pronto," called Bysidian as they ran for the door leaving the sleeping Max, Luke, Chloe and Lottie to their dreams and the three tired dragons to rest buried deep within the radiator.

CHAPTER 6

Mr Rabbit

"Steady as she goes lads, hold her now." The Swirling Pearl emerged from the clouds and scrapped along the rooftops pitching violently side to side.

As she bounced off chimney stacks the pirate crew, knee deep in cold rainwater, tried to keep her in the air. The wind whistled through the rigging and the sails thrashed wildly to free themselves from the ropes restraining them whilst hunks of hail hurtled down ripping holes in the canvas.

Solomon Fear stood at the wheel with a grip so tight his knuckles shone white. One slip and it would break free sending them crashing to the ground.

"It's here I can feel it. What did I tell you? I knew they would lead us to it if we watched them long enough," the evil captain called as he looked below for signs of his precious lost pearl.

"We have to land captain," screeched a scrawny pirate clinging onto a rope as it flung him off his feet and around the deck, "we're losing her."

As the ship's hull slid along the roof tiles a garden appeared below.

"Hold on boys I'm setting her down," called their captain as the ship slipped off the edge and plummeted towards the ground.

With an almighty splash, the ship bounced like a skipping stone across a pool of water and stopped with a crunch as it hit the base of a statue.

The wailing groans of damaged pirates could be heard above the howling wind as the lightning flashed off the building walls surrounding them.

"Drop the anchor and get those sails down, quick before we capsize," shouted Solomon Fear as the pool swirled below, "then take cover and we will ride this storm out."

As the pirates ran below deck to their squalid quarters two pirates remained to defy the storm.

"You won't beat me," hollered Solomon Fear throwing a fist to the sky at the Hail Hurlers and Wind Woozels trying to stop them.

"Can you still feel it Captain?" asked the faithful pirate by his side.

"Yes, it's here Finnegan. I don't know which one it is but it's here, the question is where?"

Solomon studied the rows of windows looking down on them. A sudden sheet of lightning illuminated the garden and at that precise moment the Goosebump

Goblin appeared in a window lit up like a beacon to the watchers below.

"There you are my friend," grinned the pirate captain as he watched the goblin vanish and the face of a small girl appear at the glass.

Through the sleeping hospital corridors, the children and their tiny visitors ran, following Snitch and his map from the Guardians library.

"Here through these doors and we need to go up the stairs but be careful we're close now the goblin could be anywhere," puffed Snitch as Max scooped him up and placed him on his shoulder.

"Phew, thanks Max I was running out of steam."

Pushing open the doors Luke listened up the towering stairwell for any signs of goblin movement.

BANG, a door slammed shut making the children leap in fright.

"That must be him up there I saw the light from an open door," said Luke.

With no dragon power to climb the giant stairs, Chloe and Lottie carefully placed Noggin and Fitz on their shoulders. Offering his hand Luke smiled at Bysidian and Templar.

"Here let me help you."

"No, no we will be just fine, after all, we are warriors, we can make these stairs no problem," insisted Bysidian running to the first step and launching himself towards it. He grabbed the top with his fingertips leaving his legs dangling below and scrabbled up awkwardly.

Loyal Templar followed, hauling himself up in his clanking armour before they ran together for the second step.

Hoisting themselves up the two suborn warriors clumsily swung their legs onto the step and clambered to their feet then ran for the next.

"Honestly are we going to have to watch you do this one step at a time," sighed Noggin getting impatient. "We don't have all night you know. Stop being so proud and admit you need a lift."

"Never," snapped Bysidian "we've got this, we fight nightmares you know."

Lottie giggled quietly trying not to offend the brave warriors as she watched them struggle.

"Is he always like this?" she asked Noggin perched on her shoulder.

"Mostly yes," replied Noggin as the armour clad warriors ran for step four and with grunts and groans dragged themselves to the top.

It all became too painful to watch.

"Going up," announced Luke as he pinched hold of the tiny black cloaks flapping around the struggling duo.

Dangling from his fingers he lifted the protesting warriors into the air and carried them up the remaining steps to the door above. As quietly as possible the other children and their tiny cargo followed.

"Well it's up here for sure," said Lottie looking at wrappers blowing around their feet and a pair of melted chocolate handprints on the handle.

"Luke, can you lift us so we can see through there?" asked Bysidian pointing towards the small pane of thick glass.

"No problem," said Luke as he lifted Bysidian and Templar to his shoulders and leant his face forward to peer through.

"I SEE YOU," screamed the goblin with a thump as his face appeared on the other side of the glass millimetres from Luke's.

"AARRGGHHH," screamed Luke as the creature pointed at him with one long yellow fingernail. Placing it on the glass it dragged the nail down making the most awful nerve tingling squeal, then ran away.

Shocked Luke stumbled backwards with Bysidian and Templar hanging onto his ear lobes to keep their footing.

"Luke are you ok?" asked Fitz looking at the visibly shaken boy trying hard to catch his breath.

"Yes, phew just startled that's all, I thought it was coming through."

Warily Chloe opened the door a crack so she and Fitz could peep into the corridors beyond.

"All clear," she whispered slipping through into the seating area inside.

With everyone safe, the tiny hitchhikers were lowered to the floor where Bysidian and Templar adjusted their armour and cloaks in a disgruntled huff.

BEEP, BEEP, BEEP

a screaming alarm pierced the air, then another and another coming from various doorways along the hall. Alerted to the danger nurses feet hammered along the floor dashing towards the alarms.

"What's that," cried Snitch as Noggin grabbed his arm and dragged him from the commotion under the safety of a waiting room seat.

"Alarms, the goblin likes the noise and chaos, so it pulls the monitor cables and sensors off the seriously ill children," replied Chloe putting her fingers in her ears.

With that, the Goosebump Goblin shot from one room and slid between a running nurse's legs into the room opposite swinging from his hand a sock stuffed full of blue light.

"Is everyone alright?" called a nurse to her colleagues.

"Yes, all ok here, I have no idea why the alarm sounded, she's sound asleep and perfectly fine," said another walking into the corridor.

"All good here as well," reported a third, "I don't understand how the sensor came off his finger in his sleep though. I guess he must have rolled onto it, but it should have stayed put."

"We'll get the monitors checked out in the morning, something odd has been happening the last few nights and what is all this mess on the floor?" asked the nurse picking up a crumpled silver foil wrapper.

The children and their tiny friends waited until the only noise was the sound of the nurse's footsteps as they left to continue their shifts.

"I can't believe it takes their hopes and wishes," sighed Chloe peeping into a room to watch a small girl with little hair sleep wrapped in warm blankets. "Of all the children here these are so sick their hopes and wishes are all they have sometimes to get them through."

"Hello Mr Rabbit, nice to see you again," said the voice of the goblin across the hallway.

"Ah Mr Goblin nice to see you too, we've been waiting for you," said the goblin waggling a stuffed toy white rabbit and speaking in a squeaky voice as if the rabbit were replying.

It was sat on the bed of a small boy who could have been no older than six by Fitz's estimation. The boy was fast asleep as the surrounding monitors beeped and flashed reporting every change from the various tubes and lines covering his tiny body.

"So Mr Rabbit what do you have for me tonight," chuckled the goblin flapping the toy's ears around.

"Well Henry here has been working hard all day on a nice juicy bunch of hopes and wishes for you," it replied as the rabbit, "Would you like to see?"

"Oh yes please, don't mind if I do," replied the goblin and tossed the stuffed toy to the floor.

Stood over the sleeping boy the Goosebump Goblin teased the blue light from Henry's nostril and held it high a look of sheer delight on its face.

"Oh well done that's a juicy one, I look forward to seeing what's inside you." Grabbing a sock from its bag it dropped the precious treasure inside.

Noggin could watch no more, "oh no you don't give that back," she yelled hurtling across the room in a blast of rage.

Snatching the grappling hook from her belt she launched it towards the bedcovers and began to climb after the goblin who started bouncing around cackling in utter delight at the little person who he knew would never catch him.

"Noggin please stop, you'll get hurt," cried Lottie standing with the others in the doorway.

"Is this what you want?" the goblin called swinging the sock around above its head as it bulged with the boy's hopes and wishes. "Well, you can have it if you catch me."

"If I catch you, I'll take more than that sock. I will make sure you are hidden in that vault where no one will ever find you again. Bysidian and his men will never banish you and you'll have to live alone in that pearl prison forever."

"Oh, threatening words from such a little lady."

"She's no lady," cried Snitch and Fitz as they ran after her Dream Catcher pearl in hand ready to produce Noggins promise.

The Goosebump Goblin was now squealing with laughter springing higher and higher on the bed when suddenly there was a startled cry. Sleeping Henry had woken from his mattress bouncing violently around.

Afraid, but unable to see the evil goblin or the tiny chasers the terrified boy began crying and fumbling for the toy rabbit he needed as comfort.

Noggin had now reached the top of the bed and was scrambling across the crumpled covers clawing to reach the creature as Snitch and Fitz watched on.

"Maybe next time crazy lady," sneered the goblin as it hastily blew a haze of blue into the air. Seizing its chance to escape the goblin sprang from the bed and launched itself at a mirror hanging above Henry's washbasin, vanishing to who knows where.

The blue dust began to waft up the boy's nostrils as he watched in sleepy amazement the rabbit lift magically from the floor and land softly on the bed beside him courtesy of invisible Chloe.

Tenderly twiddling the raggedy much loved rabbit's ear Henry drifted back to a night of restless sleep, his little body twitching as if his mind were drowning in his fears.

"That things too fast and it knows it," snapped Noggin as she joined the others in the doorway leaving a trail of small blue footsteps, "Bysidian, Templar why didn't you help, we are supposed to be here as a team remember?"

Bysidian shook his head, "Noggin chasing the goblin is not the way, it's too cunning to simply be caught by chasing it, why do you think we have so little information on them in the Guardians library?

Catching one is almost impossible, I have no idea who even caught this one in the first place. What I do know is that we have to be cleverer than it is, trickier and smarter or we don't stand a chance."

CHAPTER 7

Jellybeans and Vomit

The faint aroma of scorching dragon scales drifted across the ward as the goblin capture team walked back in.

"What do you think that blue dust does?" asked Luke, "it always blows some at them every time it leaves."

Snitch glanced at Bysidian, he knew as did Templar, he had read it in the Guardians library earlier but worrying his friends with that information was not something he was willing to do yet.

"It looks just like the dust that was in my hand after the ballerina girls hopes and wishes died," replied Max.

"Maybe it gives them a bit back, maybe it doesn't take it all and it's not as bad as we think," said Chloe who always managed to see the good in everyone.

"Don't you believe it," mumbled Snitch as he turned to walk away when he stopped and stared at the floor. Lifting his feet one by one he examined the underside of his boots. "Nope, not mine, do any of you still have wet feet?" The others shook their heads. "Then I don't think we are alone."

Two trails of small wet footprints
glistened in the brief flashes of light from
outside and they were heading for the
radiator.

"Ember, Ammolite, Argent show
yourselves," called Bysidian as they
followed the pools of water to the dragons
resting place. A scuffling of talons on the
paintwork and a squeak of leathery scales
were followed by three dozy heads.

"You're safe good. Ammolite who was
here?" asked Templar looking at his
faithful dragon for an answer.

Ammolite stared at him for a moment
with a blank look on her face then turned
to Argent and then Ember .

"You three fell asleep, didn't you?" snapped Templar, "I told you not to please tell me you saw who it was."

Bysidian crouched below the hot metal and picked up several pieces of dusty broken pearl that had been pulled from the pipe holes in the floor.

"Leave it, Templar, I know who's here and why, he's come looking for his lost pearl."

"Oh no pirates," wailed Snitch "not again please."

Noggin sat in the shadows beneath Chloe's bed listening to her sleepy soft rhythmic breathing. The others were busy talking pirates and plans but Noggin had

other things on her mind. The burning
anger still boiled inside from seeing the
goblin taking that small sick boys hopes
and wishes.

She had to find out more about this evil
creature. Where it came from, where it
vanished to and more importantly what it
wanted with all those hopes and wishes.
Then they might stand a chance of
catching it.

Noggin looked across the room at her
white haired friend, he had the answers
she was sure hidden in the Guardians
library.

Her mind flooded with questions. What
had he seen that Bysidian had stopped
him repeating? Was it the key to catching

108

the goblin? Surely Snitch would never keep that hidden, would he? Whatever he saw it wasn't like Snitch to withhold anything, he couldn't even keep the simplest secret, so it had to be bad.

"Noggin would you like one?" asked Max joining her under the bed holding out a half-eaten bag of Jellybeans from his bedside drawer. "You must be hungry I know we all are."

"Careful Noggin there are some disgusting ones hidden in there," warned Chloe as a shocked Snitch let out a wail and dropped the giant yellow bean with a chunk missing from his hands.

"Oh my life that tastes like rotten eggs, stand back I'm going to throw up."

Gagging on the vile taste he hastily removed his gloves and took off his glasses to wipe his watering eyes.

"No Snitch the ones that taste like sick are the round orange ones," laughed Luke.

Fitz quickly drop the orange ball in his hand and watched it roll away across the floor.

"Oh Chloe you spoilsport," smiled Max as he handed Noggin a multicoloured treat. "Here this one's safe its Tutti-Frutti flavoured trust me."

Noggin paused this was a boy who thought it wise to skateboard off his dads shed roof, should she trust him? Of course she should Max was like her crazy, fearless and a bit of a joker. She looked at

Chloe who nodded reassurance before taking the large bean in both hands and cautiously licked the outside.

"Delicious, thanks Max," she said with a forced smile to hide her inner anger.

Meanwhile, Snitch was in full drama queen mode ranting and raving about the revolting taste in his mouth and that's when it happened. With all the hullabaloo Noggins cunning plan suddenly hatched in her fiery redheaded mind.

"Here Snitch take a piece of mine it's yummy," she called running from below the bed and tearing a chewy piece off.

Holding it out she waited for Snitch to take it all the time looking from her eye corners at the gloves and glasses on the floor. They held the answers, all she needed was a minute they couldn't be that hard to use.

Snitch put his glasses back on so he could see the sweet treat Noggin was wafting at him.

"I don't trust you," he said it's probably Poo flavoured, or even worse Dragon Farts."

"Suit yourself grumpy pants, your loss," Noggin chirped licking her fingers and wandering away from the others.

"Imagine a Guardians toenail fluff flavour or Squidgeable Slug slime flavour. No, wait I have it Fog Flompers curly bottom hair flavour *Urgh GROSS!*"

Whilst the others were busy howling with laughter inventing new weird flavours Noggin grabbed her chance.

So as not to draw attention she casually strolled across the room towards the orange sweet Fitz had dropped. It had hair and bits of fluff stuck to the sticky shell, but it would be perfect for her plan.

Ripping off a small piece she hastily crammed it into one of her many pockets and returned to the conversation before she was missed.

At the back of the laughter filled group tucked from view Bysidian watched Noggin slip back, he knew her well enough to know when she was up to something. Being kind to Snitch was a red flag any day. What was she doing? He didn't know but one thing was for sure he would have to watch her from now on.

CHAPTER 8

Liars

Eventually, the sugar rush wore off and drained from his outburst Snitch decided to clamber into Lottie's dressing gown pocket and have a snooze.

Warm and cosy Snitch was soon snoring loudly disrupting the others intense planning on how to capture the goblin.

"Will someone please wake him up or he'll wake everyone in this place," snapped Fitz wandering around the piece of paper torn from Choles notebook holding a giant pencil he was using to draw a diagram and map.

This was Noggins chance, "I'll get him."

She dove into the pocket and crawled beside poor Snitch then reached inside her pocket and removed the orange chunk of vomit flavoured sweet.

The timing was key and as Snitch opened his mouth ready for a colossal snore in went the sweet. Slowly it began to melt, orange goo dribbled from his mouth corner and down his chin filling his mouth.

"Wake up will you," said Noggin loudly for the benefit of the others.

Snitch groaned and as he did, he automatically swallowed the mouthful of disgusting orange slop.

"And here we go," whispered Noggin with an evil smirk.

Snitch sat up abruptly deep in Lottie's pocket as a look of horror exploded onto his face.

"Let me out, let me out Noggin *move out of the way*," he screeched scrambling from the pocket with sly Noggin close behind.

"What is wrong Snitch," asked Lottie watching a green faced white haired Snitch burst out onto the floor.

"I'm going to puke," yelled Snitch clamping a hand across his salty watering mouth and running around in a panic. As the orange goo dropped into Snitch's stomach it began to grumble and churn.

"Don't worry I've got him," assured Noggin continuing the act as she grabbed his arm and lead him away from the others.
"Here Snitch take a seat you'll feel better if you stop running around, let me help you."

Snitch held out his clammy hands and scheming Noggin helped him remove his gloves and glasses before offering him the bottom of a curtain to wipe his runny eyes and mouth.

"I'm sorry Snitch but I had to," whispered Noggin as she slid the gloves onto her own hands. Snitch felt too sick to respond as he watched Noggin put on his glasses magnifying her eyes tenfold.

"*NOGGIN,*" yelled Bysidian running full steam towards her, "*DON'T YOU DO IT.*"

"Guys, what is she doing with Snitch's glasses and gloves on?" asked a puzzled Luke as Noggin bolted away from Bysidian.

"Templar grab her," yelled Bysidian as Noggin slid superhero style under a bed.

Templar gave chase but Noggin was too quick running as fast as her legs would carry her whilst dodging and swerving their grasp.

"Come on, come on," she cried clapping her gloved hands together until, "yes you beauties," as they sparked into life. "Blimey, how does he see where he's going and read all this at the same time?"

Narrowly avoiding a curtain Noggin tried desperately to get the glasses screen to work at the same time as type on the keyboard floating before her.

"Noggin what are you doing, stop," yelled Fitz charging after her but Noggin was not listening.

Zig-zagging across the room she typed

S.N.A.C.F.X....

"darn it wrong keys," she cried.

Delete, delete... C.H.E.N and

thumped the return key.

Bysidian and Templar had formed a pincer movement and were running at her from either side when an image of the creature appeared on the lens.

"STOP HER," yelled Fitz to the startled children but they were too slow to respond and Noggin slipped between their feet.

"Look at her go, she's like a mini ninja," said startled Max.

Ember poked her head from the radiator and seeing the pandemonium unfold decided the best plan of action was to avoid getting involved and return to her slumber.

"Here it comes, faster, faster," ordered Noggin anxiously as information began to scroll across one screen. Giant green eyes flickered back and forth as Noggin scanned for answers to her questions.

A tug on her belt snapped her back to the chase as Bysidian grabbed for her but lost his grip.

"Gathers hope and dreams, a creature of nightmares, blue dust blah, blah yes I know all that. Ah ha, here we go this creature is not a nightmare itself instead this is a…"

Bam! Noggin ran straight into the sheet the children had stretched out in her path stopping her instantly tangled in the fabric.

Bysidian and Templar dragged Noggin out by her kicking legs and ripped the seeker glasses of her red face.

"He's the creator of nightmares," she yelled furiously pushing their grip away and throwing the gloves to the floor. "That thing is not a nightmare from a child's imagination, it *is* the creator of those nightmares."

Fitz stopped and stared at Noggin as she erupted in anger he had never seen before.

"What did you say?"

"That thing isn't *from* a nightmare Fitz it *makes* the nightmares. All those children we help every night, this thing is there first making the nightmares we save them from. He knew, and he knew and so did he, their all liars," snapped Noggin pointing in turn to Bysidian, Templar and then Snitch who was crawling towards them feeling for his glasses. Noggin picked up the limp gloves and launched them at Snitch hitting him smack in the face.

"Hey, Noggin stop it," he protested as Bysidian handed him back his glasses. "I did not lie but hid it from you as I didn't want to scare you, I was protecting you believe it or not. Besides what difference does it make where it came from or what it does, we still have to catch it like any normal nightmare."

"I DON'T GET SCARED SNITCH," screamed back Noggin fighting hot angry tears welling in her eyes. "I thought you were part of this team, but I guess not." Her sobs began to fill the room as the tears broke their bank and poured down her cheeks.

"Where did you think the nightmares came from?" asked Bysidian.

"I DON'T KNOW," she screamed back.

All eyes were on Noggin, the children were scared. What had happened to the tiny heroes sent to save them? Why was Noggin so angry?

Fitz watched Noggin fall to pieces before him sobbing uncontrollably. He had seen this once before back when Bysidian had shown them the Nightmare vault for the first time.

"Bravo, now that's what I like to see mutiny in the ranks." A familiar voice from the doorway was applauding their fight loudly. Snitch slipped on his glasses and the first thing he focused on was

Solomon Fear and his crew member Footcheese Finnegan gloating.

"Pirates," gasped Max not sure if the tingling in his tummy was from excitement or fear.

"Oh no he's all we need, I knew we were not alone," groaned Snitch still feeling too sick to bother being scared.

"Well I see you have all met my friend and his blue dust, it's a sensational feeling isn't it Noggin when you breathe it in? All that fear it releases and it seems also anger in your case."

"How could you leave that thing in there?" demanded Bysidian walking towards his evil brother.

"Even worse how could you free it again?" added Templar standing in front of the children protectively.

"I didn't release it remember, it was that fool and his annoying butter fingered friend Nift," replied Solomon waving his cane end towards Fitz. "I would have savoured the Snacchen's release and everything it can accomplish for me but unfortunately that joy was taken out of my hands."

Bysidian sped up almost running towards the two pirates who began to back away and flee down the corridor calling out as they left.

"Tick tock little brother, the sunrise is coming and times running out. How do you catch a Snacchen, that's the question? Good luck he's a slippery little sucker."

"That thing already blames you for its lengthy imprisonment, I am sure it will be pleased to see you. Maybe we *should* let you get to it first," yelled Fitz as a door banged and the pirates disappeared.

"Erm Brother?" asked Max puzzled.

"Oh boy that's an even *longer* story," replied Snitch.

"AchOO," Noggin sneezed loudly from the strong odour of rancid cheese that followed Finnegan around.

"Excuse me," she sniffed as a haze of blue wafted from her hair and filled her damp hand.

129

"The blue dust, you must have got covered on that boy's bed when you were chasing the goblin," said Chloe handing Noggin a piece of tissue to wipe her hand.

"Oh it's my fault again, typical," snapped Noggin. Her blunt reply caught Chloe off guard and made her pull back.

"Noggin that's enough," replied Fitz, "we need to get that blue stuff off you before you say something you regret."

Noggin huffed and sat cross armed glaring at everyone she wanted to punch right there and then.

"We need to wash it off," said Luke reaching for the water jug at the nearest bedside.

"No, wait I have a better idea," smirked Snitch.

CHAPTER 9

Stinking Poopsicles

"Let me go," screamed Noggin as the icy rain pummelled against her tiny body dangling from the open window.

"Don't worry we won't drop you, but you deserve this, don't deny it," said Bysidian with a tight grasp on Noggins right leg and boot.

"We should have made you eat a piece of that orange stuff whilst you're out there, see how much you like it," added

Snitch holding onto her other leg (with Templars help as he was way too small to hold an angry Noggin alone).

With blue water running from her clothes and soaked hair Noggin wiggled and shouted, "Snitch when I get back in there, I'm going to make you sorry. I'll feed you to the Wind Woozels and then when the poo you out I'll get the Ice Imps to freeze you so you will be a huge stinking poopsicle forever."

"Boy she's angry this time that blue powder is strong stuff," said Fitz trying not to laugh.

"Ok please bring her inside now the blues gone hasn't it?" pleaded Chloe watching the upside down face of poor shivering Noggin change from red to white.

A roll of thunder was followed by a flash and *BAM!* the Goosebump Goblin burst from the window. It slipped across the ward floor trying to get its footing as it stared in shock at the unexpected group of watchers.

"It's the goblin, watch out," squealed Lottie in terror as the confused creature skid along the floor and crashed into a bed.

Noggin screamed as Snitch and Templar lost their grasp on her leg and fell from the windowsill crashing to the ground.

"I've got you Noggin hang on," yelled Bysidian as her other wet leg and boot started to slip from his hand.

"I'm falling someone help me," screamed Noggin.

Luke dashed forward and reached out of the window just as Bysidian lost his grip scooping Noggin up in his warm palm before carrying her to safety inside.

"PIRATES," yelled the goblin staring at the children one by one and pointing with a hope catching fingernail, "I smell them, Fear is here, where is he."

"Gone," replied Luke bravely, "he's gone but he's coming after you."

"Don't believe you. You're hiding him it's a trick," snapped the goblin as it began to yank the bedcovers off the sleeping Chloe, Lottie, Luke and Max and throw them to the floor.

"NO, NO, NO," yelled Fitz, "stop that thing it'll wake them up," but it was too late.

One by one the sleeping children woke to see their bed covers flying through the air and landing in piles on the ward floor.

As each woke their nightmare body vanished and as Luke disappeared Noggin dropped from his hand landing with a thud on a pile of bedcovers beneath.

"NO," cried Chloe as she sat up wide awake and placed a hand on her face feeling her scar.

"I can't see, what's happening?" called Lottie bandages around her eyes again.

"That THING woke us up," groaned Luke reaching for his leg in pain, "and I dropped Noggin I hope she's alright."

"Quick we need to get back to sleep, Fitz and the others will need us," said Max grabbing a sheet from the floor which was promptly snatched out of his hand by the invisible goblin.

"Oh no you don't you don't scare me anymore," said Max grabbing the sheet back and starting a tug of war.

Mischievous as ever the goblin waited for the right moment then let go sending Max crashing to the floor. With a thump, his cast arm hit the ground making him scream in pain.

"What on earth is happening in here?" asked the nurse dashing into the room on hearing Max's cry.

"The storm woke us up," lied quick thinking Luke, "and Lottie and Chloe were cold, so Max and I decided to give them our blankets. Max slipped on one. Sorry, it's a mess."

The nurse helped Max to his feet and into bed, "That was kind of you both but Max you need to be more careful with that arm does it hurt still?" Max shook his head. "This storm is a bad one though we were just saying it's not like any we have heard before. Sounds crazy I know but it is almost as if it's hovering over the hospital."

Having returned the blankets to their rightful owners and tucked them in the nurse closed the open window Noggin had been hanging out of moments before.

"Now if you ladies need more blankets let me know and try to sleep, I know it's hard but counting sheep always helps me," he smiled.

"Or counting pirates," whispered Max as the nurse wished them goodnight and left.

"Is he gone?" asked Chloe. Max slipped from his bed and checked outside.

"Yes, why?"

139

"Here take these," she said slipping from her covers and handing everyone two round white balls of cotton wool from her medicine drawer.

"These are yours for your face cream, why do we need them," asked Lottie confused.

"What are we supposed to do throw them at the goblin?" asked Luke rudely.

"No idiot put them in your ears to block out the storm, we don't want to risk anything waking us up again."

For what seemed like an eternity the four children tossed and turned trying to sleep. The thunder seemed louder, the lightning brighter and the wind howled as if the storm were keeping them awake on purpose. Watching the rhythmic movement of the ceiling light swing back and forth (the goblin was using it as a swing to keep away from the tiny people below) Chloe's vision began to blur as one by one the children returned to their friends.

"Noggin are you alright," cried Luke searching for her everywhere.

"I'm fine." The muffled voice came from Lottie's bed as a small lump crawled towards the top and out popped a mass of red hair. "That nurse swooped me up with the bed covers. You all remembered us when you woke up, how can that be no child ever remembers us?"

"Of course we remembered you how could we forget this crazy bunch?" said Luke relieved Noggin was unhurt.

Snitch was sat in a heap on the ward floor cut and bruised from his fall with Templar, he was shaken, and one side of his glasses had a crack in them, but he was alright.

"Ripped from the nightmare," he mumbled.

"What did you say?" asked Noggin abruptly.

"They remembered us because they were ripped from the nightmare, we didn't capture it and leave them a happy dream like normal, that thing woke them up," he said pointing to the goblin on the light.

"And how exactly do you know that?" asked Noggin already knowing the answer and poised ready to jump on Snitch's reply.

"It's in the Guardians library," he tutted knowing full well what Noggin was fishing for.

"Oh so now you decide to tell me what's written in there, how awfully kind of you."

Meanwhile, Bysidian and Templar circled the room on Ammolite and Argent trying to stop the goblin from escaping back through the window or out the door.

"This is it Fitz, the element of surprise, take the shot," called Bysidian.

Fitz knelt in the centre of the room and reached inside his backpack. Pulling out a milky white Dream Catcher pearl he held it high and braced for impact.

"You may want to find something to hold onto, AND DON'T LET GO," shouted Noggin to the confused children as she ran to help Snitch.

Fitz ripped open the pearl releasing an icy blast of wind that exploded into the room. A tremendous boom of thunder filled the sky outside as the storm intensified showing its fury.

The children dove for the safest place they knew, under the beds as the wind grew stronger inside their room. A sucking and gurgling sound began, quiet at first but getting louder and louder until their ears rang.

"NO," screamed the goblin dangling from the ceiling light being almost stretched in two. "I am not going back inside there, never again."

Bysidian and Templar were being thrown violently around on their rides so as the dragons made a swift dive for inside the radiator the two Night Warriors leapt from their backs and ran to help Fitz.

"Arghhh I can't hold it much longer, that things so strong," called Fitz his feet beginning to lift off the floor as the

Dream Catcher pearl pulled him towards the defiant goblin.

Bysidian and Templar braced against the wind head and shoulders down until they reached Fitz and grabbed a leg each.

"We've got you Fitz just don't let that creature go now this could be our only chance."

THUD! the goblins raggedy bag dropped past Fitz and hit the floor narrowly missing the warriors before being blown towards the door.

"*NO MY TREASURE*," screamed the goblin, "*GIVE IT BACK.*"

"Let go and come get it yourself," shouted Bysidian hanging onto Fitz as he lifted further off the floor.

"Whoa, someone help me."

Snitch whizzed across the floor dragging Noggin with him and directly in their path stood Bysidian and Templar holding onto flying Fitz.

"Sticky gloves, sticky gloves come on," yelled Noggin reaching into her pocket and throwing everything out. Tools, potions, ropes and even a pirates eyeball rolled onto the floor.

"That's an eyeball," shrieked Snitch in disgust.

"Found it on the beach at Cloud Bay," Noggin said. "It must have fallen from the pirate ship when those chickens legged it from the island last time we met. I thought it may come in handy one day."

SLAP! she slammed one gloved hand down and stopped both Snitch and her in their tracks.

"I've got you hold on," she cried as Snitch flew like a kite by one arm as Noggin wrestled to keep him safe with the other.

The light fitting above began to groan as it struggled to stay attached to the ceiling when suddenly a shrill screeching sound of nails dragging on metal filled the room.

"It's slipping," yelled Fitz, "Templar the goblins coming hold on."

The storm outside raged in anger as the creature began to lose its grip, with a look of terror and pain on its face, the goblin looked down towards Fitz.

"I SAID NO," it screamed and launched itself through the air. Like a trapeze artist, the goblin swung from curtain runner to curtain runner and rolled out of the door grabbing its precious bag of hopes and wishes as it escaped.

"ARRGGHHHH!!!!" screamed Fitz in anger as he slammed the pearl shut stopping the wind instantly. He dropped, exhausted to the floor on top of Bysidian and Templar. "What just happened, I have never seen anything escape a Dream Catcher pearl before, ever."

Bysidian stood and offered a helping hand to Templar, "I have no idea Fitz I thought they were inescapable as well, but this thing just isn't like any normal nightmare you catch."

"Is it safe to come out now?" asked Luke as the children peered from beneath the bed still holding tightly to a heavy metal leg each.

"Yes, it's safe," said Templar beckoning them out, "are you all okay anyone hurt?"

"No we're all fine," said Max rubbing his sore plastered arm as they crawled from hiding.

"I thought you had the goblin then, that pirate Solomon was right it is one slippery little sucker."

"Thank the Guardians for your sticky gloves Noggin, I thought we were all ..." Bysidian stopped.

A lone black sticky glove was lying limp on the floor, Noggin and Snitch were gone.

CHAPTER 10

A World of Nightmares

Buried deep inside the goblins sock stuffed bag Noggin and Snitch bounced around as it ran.

"Why did you do that, this is not a good plan at all Noggin what if it finds us and eats us?" whispered Snitch crossly pushing a smelly used sock from his face. Yet again he had been dragged into one of

Noggins schemes and he was not best pleased.

"Shush, stop moaning will you this way we can find out where it goes but we won't if it finds us first so be quiet."

"What are you going to do when we get wherever the goblins going, jump out and shout surprise, that's not going to do the trick believe me," continued Snitch annoyed at being dragged into Noggins schemes again.

"I haven't got that far Snitch, but I'll think of something trust me."

"Trust you, how can I trust you ever again Noggin you tricked me and stole my glasses and gloves. You made me eat vomit sweets."

"Didn't you hear Solomon, that was the blue dust, not me?"

"Oh no, the dust made you mad and angry but the trickery, that was all you Noggin as per usual."

"Okay I'm sorry but I had to, you were hiding things we needed to know and now we will get some answers if you just keep quiet."

From deep within the socks a blue light began to glow, another then another as the trapped hopes and wishes called out to the stowaways for help.

Noggin pulled the sock out she was sitting on and opened the top to peep inside. A beautiful blue light danced and sparkled as gentle voices called out in desperation. Slowly she began to reach inside when Snitch grabbed her arm.

"No stop don't touch it remember what happened when Max held that girls it died," reminded Snitch.

Noggin withdrew her hand quickly and folded over the top of the sock sadness in her eyes.

"They sound so unhappy Snitch there must be something we can do to help them escape."

"What can we do though, we can't just leave them lying around randomly hoping the right children find them."

"No not the right children but the right people, that's it oh I could kiss your chubby little cheeks sometimes."

"Ugh, I'd rather you didn't if it's all the same to you and less of the chubby, anyway what did I say?"

Noggin grabbed the top of the nearest glowing sock, "here help me tie this up and I'll explain."

With the best knot tied they could manage with their tiny hands Noggin and Snitch hoisted the sock to the top of the bag. Once they were sure the goblin wasn't looking out it went, and they watched the sock vanish into the distance lying on the corridor floor

"Are you sure about this?" whispered Snitch, "what if they don't find it?"

"Come on Snitch this is Fitz, Bysidian and Templar, they must be missing us by now. They'll find it trust me now grab the next one."

"They were right here," said Bysidian pulling at Noggins sticky glove until it eventually relinquished its hold and slurped off the floor.

"Well they aren't now are they," said Fitz. "It's Noggin we are talking about she could be anywhere, and she's dragged poor Snitch with her yet again."

"Maybe they got sucked inside that pearl of yours?" said Max.

"No nothing went inside believe me, not even the thing that was supposed to," huffed Fitz.

"The bag," gasped Lottie.

"Oh you have to be kidding me," said Fitz, "she wouldn't?"

"Yes, she would, and you know it," replied Templar rolling his eyes.

"So they could be anywhere with that thing out there pulling blue hope bogies from children's noses. How on earth are we supposed to find them?"

"Shush listen, do you hear that?" hushed Lottie who was now stood in the doorway peeping out into the corridor beyond.

Joining her the others listened as the two arguing voices became clearer the closer, they got.

"Pull harder will you, I can't move this thing back to the ship by myself."

"I can't believe our luck captain, imagine us finding it just lying on the floor like that calling for help."

"Luck has nothing to do with it Finnegan, destiny is what it's called as I always tell you. We may not have that darn Snacchen yet, but this will do nicely for now. I just have to figure out what it does with them, and I won't need that creature anymore. How difficult can it be?"

Around the bend, two tiny figures dressed in tatty black long coats appeared dragging a blue twinkling sock.

"I have to stop captain for a second I need a breather," said Footcheese Finnegan puffing with exhaustion.

"Come on man where is your pirate grit," snapped Solomon Fear secretly relieved to have a break himself.

That strange feeling of being watched wafted over the pirates and turning around they saw the children, Fitz, Bysidian and Templar staring at them.

"I don't believe that belongs to you," said Bysidian pointing at the sock.

"Finders keepers," cackled Footcheese.

"That's right Finnegan, we found it and that means it does," said Solomon drawing his sword and standing his ground.

"If you want it come and get it or you could be sensible and just let us leave with our treasure without any trouble."

160

"Oh please," said Luke walking towards the tiny pirates, "I'm a thousand times the size of you what is that sword going to do to me?"

Picking up the sock Luke watched them run in a flurry of black moth eaten coats and clattering swords.

"Yeh not so brave now are you," he called after them.

"Wait," yelled Bysidian dashing after them, "where did you find that sock?"

"None of your business," yelled back Solomon running for the double doors blocking his way.

"Yeah, we didn't drag it all the way through those doors at the end and down the other corridor for nothing," shouted

Footcheese Finnegan a proud smirk on his face.

"You idiot," snapped Solomon thwacking him around the back of the head as they pushed one door open a crack just enough to make their escape.

Max began to laugh, "Are pirates always that stupid?"

"Not all of them, only a special few," grinned Bysidian. Ask Fitz to tell you about Boz-eyed Bert and Three Toes Magee sometime."

Cradling the sock safely in his hands Luke pushed open the swing doors and looked along the seemingly endless corridor stretched out before him.

"He said they found it at the end of here."

"Then down there we go," said Fitz striding through the doors.

The corridor lights hummed in the quiet as the band of goblin chasers made their way to where the sock was found. Door after door leading to a maze of corridors the air was filled with the smell only hospitals have and the lingering odour of mouldy parmesan courtesy of Footcheese Finnegan.

"Does anyone else think it's odd the goblin dropped a sock, after all, it seems so protective over them?" asked Max.

"Oh it doesn't even know it lost one believe me," replied Fitz as they reached the end of the corridor and stood wondering which direction to go.

"Noggin may be a pain in the backside and drive us around the bend sometimes, but she knows when to show us the way."

"But which way?" asked Lottie looking left then right.

"Hang on something odd's happening with this sock," said Luke holding it out in his palm. The glow grew stronger and the voices began to call louder and louder.

"Hold it this way," instructed Bysidian pointing to the right hand corridor. Luke did as he was asked and watched as the light dimmed and the voices faded. "Now this way," asked Bysidian pointing left. Luke's hand began to glow blue and the voices returned.

"They're showing us the way," gasped Lottie.

Along the left corridor, they ran and there on the floor, another sock.

"Hey that's one of mine," said Luke picking up a green sock covered in black and white footballs.

Gathering the sock stuffed with hopes and wishes Chloe placed it in her dressing gown pocket for safekeeping.

"Don't worry we will get you back where you belong," she promised.

Two more socks later they were deep inside the huge hospital away from Luke,

Max, Chloe and Lottie's ward and the dragons fast asleep in the radiator.

Suddenly a familiar voice shouted.

"Blah yuck," followed by loud spitting noises.

The sound of cutlery crashing to the floor and drinks machines gurgling led the team to the visitors coffee shop.

Lying under the soda machine was the goblin, a steady stream of fizzy cola pouring into its mouth. The more it drank the more its tummy grew until…

BURRRRRPPPPPP!!!!!

Scattered on the floor were half eaten sandwiches and ready-made salads.

"Oh dear healthy stuff, it'll hate that," whispered Chloe.

After releasing the gassy drink from its tummy the goblin discovered, much to its delight the cakes and sweets section.

Large handfuls of chocolate cake, cookies and pie were shovelled into its mouth and when it found the hot chocolate on tap, it was in heaven.

Swinging from its side throughout were Noggin and Snitch hidden inside the bag.

"I don't feel so good," whined Snitch after all the rocking around.

"Here place your head between your knees and wrap yourself in this thick fluffy sock," said Noggin helpfully.

"Will it make me feel better?" asked Snitch

"No but it will muffle your voice, so I don't have to hear you whine," said Noggin scrabbling up the bag and peeping out to see where they were.

"See I told you to trust me they found us," she reported back to sickly Snitch. "The others are just outside I told you they would follow the socks."

All of a sudden, the goblin stopped and removing its head from beneath the hot chocolate machine sat bolt upright sniffing the air. The milky brown fluid ran from its mouth as it looked around.

"I've been waiting for you *liar*," it said calmly.

"Liar?" mouthed Fitz to Bysidian and Templar thinking the goblin meant them.

"Well that's no way to greet an old friend," replied Solomon Fear appearing a distance from the others.

"Old friend don't make me laugh," snapped the goblin landing on the floor before the pirates. "You said you would come back for me, you said you would free me, LIAR."

"I'm no liar, you're free now and I'm here so I did as I promised," said Solomon Fear hands out to calm the upset creature.

"NO liar," the goblin screeched spitting brown fluid everywhere. "If you had freed me you would have been there when the pearl smashed open and I escaped."

"I planned to be but there were complications of the Dream Drifter kind. They tried to steal you for their personal use, I saved you sending the pearl to Earth before they could get their grubby hands on it. Now I'm here to carry out my promise, you and me working together as a team to destroy the Dream Drifters, Night Warriors, Guardians and the almighty High Minister himself."

The Goosebump Goblin paused, "destroy them?"

"Yes, my evil friend. With your powers, we can create a world of nightmares. Imagine all that pain and suffering for the feeble children. Their fears would come alive with just one visit from us. You gather the hopes and wishes, create the dust and we can do the rest it's simple.

The pathetic Dream Drifters would be overpowered, meaning we could do whatever we wished. If we control the nightmares, we can terrify their little minds.

Sleepless nights means exhausted adults means we get to steal whatever we wish right under their sleep deprived noses."

"World of nightmares," repeated the goblin drumming his nails on the countertop and eyeing Solomon Fear with distrust. "Are you sure this will destroy the High Minister?"

"Yes, I promised you before and I do again, the nightmares will become too many and the vault will not be able to hold them. They will overpower the High Minister and his Guardians."

The goblins yellow teeth appeared as it smirked.

"I told him he would be sorry, all those years ago when he locked me away for good, I warned him of the consequences. There may be others like me out there but an imprisoned Snacchen is an angry Snacchen and that you do not want on your hands. Count me in."

Noggin and Snitch stared at each other in disbelief. The High Minister had caught this creature himself and now he was going to pay the price, they all were.

Solomon Fear rubbed his grimy hands together in glee.

"Excellent my friend. We are going to need as much blue dust as you can make, so we will leave you to enjoy your fun this evening. I see you have been busy already," he pointed to the bag stuffed with socks and Noggin and Snitch. "The Swirling Pearl and my crew are waiting outside on the water by the statue so as soon as your work is done, we will meet you there."

The scheming captain began to walk away, "Oh and as you may be aware there are a team of wearisome Dream Drifters, some interfering kids and a couple of useless Night Warriors somewhere around here looking for you so be careful, we wouldn't want you inside one of those Dream Catcher pearls again, now would we?"

The goblin shook his head madly licking a blob of apple pie filling from his nose tip with his long slimy tongue.

Solomon Fear vanished his work and false promises done and returned to The Swirling Pearl to await the goblins delivery of blue powder.

"I can get him, let me go," said Fitz struggling against Bysidian and Templars grasp a Dream Catcher pearl in hand.

"No, think Fitz think of Noggin and Snitch they would be trapped with that thing forever," said Templar.

In utter anger and frustration, Fitz punched his arms free and took a few steps back staring at the others as if he were going to erupt like a volcano.

"Fitz how about we just stay calm and think for a moment," said Bysidian.

"Not a chance," yelled Fitz and he shot past them running out into the open for the goblin to see.

"Don't you ever give up?" screeched the goblin in delight as he grabbed a tray and using it as a sledge slid along the service counter.

Two pairs of scared eyes peered out of his bag as Fitz watched Noggin and Snitch disappear along with the goblin through the large glass window into the darkness beyond.

CHAPTER 11

Secret Ingredients

A tummy trembling rush of weightlessness came over Snitch and Noggin as they leapt with the goblin through the reflection on the glass. Every hair on their tiny bodies stood on end like static had surged through them before they landed with a bump.

There was no longer rain or wind just quiet and the sound of running feet thudding on the ground. Noggin peeped out to see a cloudless sky filled with a million stars and breathe in the air heavy with wildflower scent from the meadow below the goblin's feet.

Glow worms scattered as he ran through the long grass following a worn path deep into a forest where a small moss covered cabin stood, a solitary orange light flickering in the window.

"Snitch look," whispered Noggin as they grew closer, "this must be its home."

The goblin jumped onto the rickety wooden porch and opening the creaking wooden door stepped inside.

The lonely cabin consisted of one small room with a single comfy old armchair and a mattress piled with blankets on the floor by a low glowing fire. The goblin threw on another log making the fire pop and crackle sending sparks up the chimney into the night sky.

Taking off the heavy bag it hooked the strap over the armchair and walked to a large workbench covered in jars of various sizes. Sleepily it slumped into an uncomfortable looking chair on wheels and sighed.

"Quick let's go," said Noggin grabbing Snitch and dragging him from the bag just in time.

As they tumbled into the bundle of blankets on the mattress the goblin reached for its bag and began to pull out the remaining socks.

To Noggin and Snitch's astoundment, the cabin ceiling began to shimmer blue as one by one thousands of hope and wishes filled socks began to glow from their place hanging on the ceiling.

"Noggin look at them all," whispered Snitch, "they cover the entire roof."

Tiny scared voices crying for help filled the small room until BANG! The goblin could take no more and slammed his hand down on the bench making the jars wobble and rattle.

"Quiet," it demanded loudly, and the voices stopped. "Now, where are you?" it mumbled as it rummaged around in the bag "I know you are in here somewhere."

A look of delight filled its wicked face as it pulled out the sock filled with the small rabbit boy Henry's hope and wishes.

"Here you are my beauty, you could finally be the one I can feel it in my bones."

"The one, what does he mean the one?" asked Snitch.

"Shush will you and we will find out," replied Noggin watching the goblin with wide eyed curiosity.

Carefully the goblin opened the sock and peered inside illuminating its face with blue light. Its usual scowl faded away leaving a look of happiness spread across every feature as its eyes glistened in delight. The evil face so harsh and cruel had vanished and a gentle soul took its place.

Delicately it reached inside and with tender care slid the blue bead of Henrys hopes and wishes free from the sock.

Cupping the light in both hands as if it may break the goblin beamed from ear to ear as it spread its trembling hands and placed the bead on the bench.

The small room exploded with blue light darting here and there as Henrys hopes and wishes finally danced free. The small cabin became alive with a cheering crowd inside a huge stadium who were all

182

watching Henry on stage playing his guitar and singing with all his might. TV cameras rolled, huge screens flickered, and photographers cameras flashed as millions of people around the globe watched Henry and his band.

"A rock star," said Noggin smiling "Henry wants to be a rock star."

The audience loved him and with a leap of faith, Henry jumped into the crowd of people being passed above their heads before being fed back to the stage all the while still singing his heart out.

The goblin jumped from his chair bursting with excitement and began to dance around the room trying to grab Henry's hand and throwing itself into the imaginary crowd. It played the air guitar with the band on stage and waved at people, but no one saw it.

'Hey, look at me I'm here don't you love me too?" it cried out at the front row who were dancing wildly but they ignored the goblin, all eyes were on Henry.

"No please, no wait," cried the goblin as its beaming face fell into despair. The blue light began to dim and one by one the people in the crowd began to fade away as the music became quieter and Henry's band disappeared.

The goblin ran to the bench and desperately scooped up the blue orb. "Please no don't die, please stay," it begged with tears in its eyes as the light faded away and the room fell quiet.

Orange and red from the crackling fireplace flickered across the goblins back and in the warm light, Noggin and Snitch watched the creatures head and shoulders drop as it began to sob.

"Why is it crying, I don't understand," whispered Noggin to Snitch. As she spoke the goblin reached out his empty hand and grabbed a jar half full of blue dust.

"It's like I told Max," Snitch replied, "It wasn't the goblins to keep, it was Henry's hopes and wishes, so they died."

Opening its hand the goblin stared at its palm now full of blue dust before slamming it hard down on top of the jar dropping the dust inside.

"Should have known," it snapped screwing on the lid as anger replaced its sadness. "They all leave me, no friends no dreams nobody wants a share with a Snacchen."

"Noggin what are you doing it's going to see you?" hissed Snitch as Noggin crawled from the blankets and stepped out onto the cabin floor in full view.

"*He* Snitch not *it*, he has feelings you know he's not a thing but a person with a soul. Can't you see that now?"

Noggin took a deep breath, "You're just lonely, aren't you?" she said to the goblin.

The goblin whizzed around on his chair to see Noggin staring at him in the firelight.

"How did you get in here? You're a thief here to steal my treasures get out," he shouted scrambling up onto the bench and knocking over several jars sending them rolling to the floor.

"We're not here to steal anything," said Snitch crawling from his hiding place to join Noggin. "These so called treasures of yours, do you know what they are?"

"I know," snapped the goblin crossly sliding from the bench to stand before them. "Hopes and wishes, special things those children have in their heads, but they don't deserve."

"Don't deserve, why?" asked Noggin.

"They don't share, they don't want me to see them that's why they die. They want them for themselves and that's not fair," he replied wiping away a stray tear and the wet from the end of his nose. "That's why I make the dust to make them sad and scared just like me."

"Not fair, why should you have their hopes and wishes don't you have some of your own?" questioned Snitch frowning.

"Don't know how," muttered the goblin quietly dropping his shoulders with sadness returning to his eyes.

"You don't know how to have your own hopes and wishes?" repeated Noggin, "oh how sad."

188

The goblin snivelled and began to busy himself picking up his stray jars placing them back on the bench.

"I just want to be part of their fun, have friends like they do and be special."

"But stealing their hopes and wishes and making this nightmare dust is not the right way to make friends or be special," added Noggin rolling a stray jar towards the goblin.

"Noggin be careful don't get any of that dust on you, I don't want to be eating vomit sweets ever again thanks."

"Oh, that won't hurt you," said the goblin to Snitch grabbing the jar, "that's just the start I have to add my own secret mixture to it before it gets nasty."

The goblin pointed to a small wooden box on the mantlepiece above the fire.

"That's the Snacchen secret ingredient passed down from generations, without that the dust is just dust."

"What's in it," asked Snitch curiously

"My mixture is made of ground toenails, tooth mould, belly button and bum fluff, ear wax and a few other delicious things I can't tell."

"Nice," said Snitch screwing up his face, "and you breathed that in," he giggled at Noggin, "serves you right."

Noggin ignored the comment, "you do know that Solomon Fear and his pirates are not to be trusted, they are not your friends."

"Of course I do, I trust him as much as your friends trust me, but he will let me stay free as long as I make him the dust. That way one day I might find the special hope and dream that doesn't die, and I get to share forever."

"Your special ingredient, does he know about that?" asked Noggin pointing at the elusive box.

The goblin shook his head, "no nobody knows only a Snacchen and of course you two now. We each have our own special mixtures so no two are the same."

"That's interesting," said Noggin tapping her finger on her lips, a plan was brewing and that made Snitch nervous.

CHAPTER 12

A Second Chance

"Anywhere," yelled Fitz angrily, "they could be anywhere by now, when we find them Noggin is in for a stonking piece of my mind."

"Calm down Fitz please you're scaring me," begged Lottie watching Fitz pacing around faster and faster. Bysidian and Templar had gone in search of the pirates leaving the children and Fitz alone.

BAM! The goblin jumped through the window he had left by only minutes earlier.

"There it is, grab that thing, do not let it go," yelled Fitz to the children as he reached for a Dream Catcher pearl and ran towards the goblin ready to rip it open.

"STOP FITZ NO," cried Noggin and Snitch jumping from the goblins bag and standing protectively on the floor between them.

"What on earth are you doing, stand aside," shouted Fitz ,"let me put that thing back where it should be."

"Listen to her Fitz," said Snitch running towards his leader, "let Noggin explain please he's not what you think."

"So do you think you can help us?" asked Noggin looking at the four children.

"Sure everyone deserves a second chance," said Luke looking at the goblin who was watching at a safe distance.

"I don't know," said Fitz, "how do we know we can trust him, he could have been working with Solomon Fear all along for all we know."

"See, see," cried the goblin dragging piles of glowing socks from his bag, "I brought them all back, everyone I have left."

"What are you going to do with them exactly?" asked Max suspiciously, "they are no use now."

"Yes, yes put them back," said the goblin. "I can put them back for the children still here, I remember where everyone came from, they can all have them back."

"Prove it," demanded Fitz, "you put them all back and we will help you."

The goblin nodded frantically "thank you, thank you but I will need some help there are too many to do alone."

"So how exactly do I do this again?" whispered Lottie stood at a sleeping girls bedside holding a glittering unicorn sock in her hand.

"Like this watch," said the goblin as he dropped a glowing blue bead into the ear of the boy he was standing over. For a moment it lay there in the poor boy's earhole not moving but with a gradual slurp, it dropped inside.

"Mustn't touch it remember, just drop it inside no hands."

Ward beyond ward, child after child the goblin and his helpers returned all the hopes and wishes they could, being careful to return them to their rightful owners.

"The last one," sighed a relieved Chloe as she dropped the final blue light into the ear of the boy in the ward next to theirs.

"What do we do with all these empty socks now?" asked Max pulling a great handful from his pyjama pockets.

"This way follow me," beckoned the goblin running down the corridor towards his favourite vending machine. Pulling it away from the wall he pointed to the back. "In here, see I keep them here for emergencies."

The entire back of the machine was stuffed full of odd socks every colour, shape and size possible. There were so many they spilt out onto the floor leaving the goblin to jam them back in with his hands and feet before sliding the machine back into place.

"Please tell me you're not going to make me take these back as well, I can't remember who they all belong to," he pleaded.

"Hopes and wishes returned, check," said Luke walking back into their familiar room, "what's next?"

"Next is the part where we have to trust you," said Noggin looking into the goblin's eyes. The goblin nodded slowly. "You remember where he said to meet them?"

"Yes," replied the goblin checking the tiny glass jar was still safely in his bag lid on tight.

"Good luck," added Snitch.

Across the beds, he bounced and with an almighty leap vanished through the window. The others dashed to the window just in time to see the goblin land in the gardens below. The rain soaked him in a flash as he looked towards the window then ran into the bushes.

"I have a bad feeling about this," muttered Fitz.

"Finally my friend you found us," called Solomon Fear staggering across the Swirling Pearls deck as she lashed side to side in the storm.

"A promise is a promise," said the goblin holding out the wet jar full of blue dust. Solomon Fear grinned taking his prize and holding it high.

"So much fear in one small jar," he cried delighted "do you have more?"

"In that jar is enough pain and suffering to last you for years, minute amounts that's all it takes," replied the goblin. "You have your dust Solomon so now there is a change of plan, I want my freedom."

Solomon Fear looked at the goblin.

"That was not the deal, what if I need more, if you leave then how will I get it?"

"Simple you find me, you get more. Of course, if you don't want any then I will take that back," the goblin said reaching for the jar in the pirate's hand.

"No wait let's not be hasty," Solomon thought for a moment.

The goblin could not be trusted he knew that. In his hands was years' worth of dust he would have riches beyond his dreams and the High Minister and Guardians destroyed. He didn't need the goblin any longer all he needed was the dust in that jar.

"Enjoy your freedom, my evil friend, you've earned it."

The goblin nodded in thanks and turned to walk away, "you're no friend of mine."

"Do you see him yet?" asked Snitch as Lottie looked through the window to the gardens below.

"Let's face it he's not coming back," said Fitz "He's fooled you Noggin, he's fooled all of us."

"Now that's where you're wrong," smiled Lottie moving swiftly from the window as BAM the goblin landed on the floor dripping wet and shivering from the cold.

"So, did he fall for it?" asked Noggin.

"Bah, friend," he said, "he is no one's friend he is just a greedy swindler and a cheat," said the goblin "well he got what he wanted."

"Dust?" said Snitch smiling.

"Yes, just dust, no special ingredient, completely useless," said the goblin grinning wickedly.

"What happens if he comes looking for you when he realises?" asked Max concerned.

"He can look all he wants, I will know when he is here pirates smell bad to Snacchens especially that pongy cheesy one. He will never get near me without me knowing first."

"Look, they're leaving," cried Luke face against the window. Over the rooftop, The Swirling Pearl sailed pirates hanging from its wind lashed sails and a lone figure at the wheel.

"Where do you think he's going?" asked Chloe as the ship vanished from view.

"To find the other pearls no doubt," replied Fitz "It's not the last we have seen of those pirates believe me."

"Fitz are you here?" Bysidian and Templar ran into the room.

"Oh Noggin, Snitch thank the heavens you're safe, the Snacchens back it gave Solomon a jar of nightmare blue dust we have to stop them. Argent. Ammolite wake up right now we have to fly."

Banging on the radiator with his sword to wake the sleeping dragons Bysidian turned and stopped mid swing.

"Nobody move the goblin is standing right there," he pointed with the sword tip.

Slowly the goblin moved to hide behind Chloe, "Bysidian put the sword away, he's our friend now."

"Friend," whispered the goblin melting with happiness at that simple word that meant so much.

Outside the storm died, the wind faded away and the rain stopped. Heavy black clouds gave way to a glistening silver full moon that shone through the window and onto the beds full of sleeping children.

"Noggin what exactly have you done?"

A long story later and after much convincing the two Night Warriors finally dropped their swords.

"You are telling me that all those nightmares were created just because he does not know how to have his own hopes and wishes?" summarised Bysidian in disbelief. "How selfish."

"The High Minister is expecting a full Nightmare Pearl when we return you know that don't you?" added Templar. "We have to take him back however changed you claim he is."

The Goosebump Goblin hung his head in shame. He was not the only Snacchen, there were hundreds creating nightmares that the Dream Drifters had to save children from every night. The others may continue being selfish and mean they didn't understand, but he could change.

"Please, all he needs is a chance," pleaded Lottie.

"We can help him," added Luke, "at least let us try."

"Yes, we can teach him how to dream and have hopes and wishes of his own," promised Chloe and Max.

"I wouldn't want to be in your shoes when my annoying brother discovers that dust is a fake, he will come looking for you and if he finds you, I have no idea what he'll do."

The goblin waved a bare knobbly foot in the air.

"Don't wear shoes so don't worry about me."

"And what exactly are we supposed to tell the High Minister when we return empty handed," asked Templar. "Those Dream Catcher pearls don't just turn black for nothing and they have a certain weight you know. Nightmares are not light."

Noggin coughed and stepped forward.

"I have a plan."

"Why does that not surprise me," sighed Bysidian. "Come on then out with it."

The goblin looked at the round orange sweet in his palm before sniffing it suspiciously.

"Not chocolate?" he said to Noggin who was standing willing him to put it in his mouth.

"Trust me it's fine, all you have to do is pop it in and let it melt. You'll like it."

Snitch shuddered as he remembered his encounter with the jellybean and a familiar slight salty taste rose in his mouth.

Putting his faith in Noggin the goblin dropped in the sweet and everyone took a step back.

"Noggin are you sure this is wise?" asked Fitz.

"Too late now," she replied as the goblin's eyes grew wider savouring the taste.

Everyone watched waiting for the goblin to explode with the vile vomit flavour but to their surprise, a grin spread across his face.

"Delicious, more," he said as a blob of orange slop hit the floor.

"That's downright gross," wailed Snitch.

"Fitz get ready and remember only a tiny crack on the count of three," reminded Noggin.

The goblin knelt before Fitz one finger raised as he concentrated on the medley of noises erupting from his stomach. A loud gurgle came from deep inside followed by a swishing and churning as the orange goo did its job.

The goblin looked at Fitz and nodded,
one finger became two, then three and
Fitz cracked open his Dream Catcher
pearl just a slither. A loud whistle escaped
and screamed around the room as the
goblin leant forward and

BURRRRRPPPPPP!!!!!

Straight into the opening.

"Quick close it before it escapes,"
called Noggin as Fitz closed the pearl and
dropped it on the floor.

"Well it's certainly heavy," he said
moving away. "I hope this works Noggin
if it blows up, we will all be sorry."

The poor small milky white pearl
rocked a little, back and forth not

knowing which way to go as the goblin gassy burp expanded inside.

"Look I think it's working," said Snitch.

Slowly the milky white turned insipid grey before becoming a dense black that swirled inside the hard shell.

Fitz picked up the newly created fake Nightmare Pearl and examined it carefully. Bouncing it up and down in one hand he judged the weight.

"Close enough, it would fool me."

"I cannot believe I've let you talk me into this," said Bysidian "If the High Minister ever found out we would both lose our roles as Night Warriors."

"Then don't tell him," said Noggin as she watched Fitz drop the burp filled pearl into his backpack.

Beyond the window, bird song filled the air as the dawn chorus welcomed the new day.

"Time to go sleepy heads," said Bysidian banging on the radiator to wake the snoozing dragons.

"Now be good," ordered Noggin jumping aboard Ember, "and listen to what the children say that way you will always have friends."

"I will I promise," replied the goblin taking hold of Chloe's hand.

"We'll look after him don't worry," reassured Luke.

"I'll miss you," sniffed Lottie trying not to cry.

"Me too, will we see you again," asked Max.

"You can count on it, we will see you many times again but whether you remember us well that's a different story," said Snitch.

"As long as there are dreams and nightmares we are always here," said Noggin as Ember rose into the air her three passengers safely seated.

Luke opened the window from the start of their adventure and the three dragons flew out into the morning sky.

"Good luck finding the other lost pearls," he called, "and watch out for those pirates."

Waving until they were out of sight, the tiny band of heroes headed into the sunrise tinged clouds leaving four tired children and a happy goblin watching from below.

"Time to wake up soon," said Luke sitting on the end of his bed being careful not to sit on his sleeping bodies toes.

"Wake up, no you will leave me all alone," cried the goblin looking scared.

"Oh no you'll not be alone, you will never be alone again," promised Chloe. "Just because we can't see you when we are awake doesn't mean we don't know you are there. We will be back tonight right here, and we can start working on those hopes and wishes together."

Warm morning sunlight woke the children in their beds and the sleeping ones faded away but as promised the goblin did not feel alone.

Visitors in the day came and went chatting and telling the children stories of the outside world. The goblin (or George as they decided to call him) sat patiently on their beds listening to every word excited to hear the tales and dream of many things he had yet to see.

Night-time fun with his new friends made blue sparkles flicker from his nose when he sneezed, his own hopes and wishes making him dance in delight.

The children saved him every vomit flavoured sweet they had and the horrible green jelly they were given for dessert with their meals.

Socks still vanished, vending machines emptied and the staff's milk and butter still had suspicious yellow and green bits in them as they were habit's the goblin struggled to change.

Over time one by one Luke, Chloe, Max then Lottie all went home to their families, but the goblin was not forgotten.

217

As one left a new friend appeared in their place bringing new stories and dreams for him to explore and create his own hopes and wishes forever.

"So you met a Snacchen?" asked the High Minister holding the Nightmare Pearl in his hands.

"Yes, High Minister and all we have heard is true, they are evil creatures," lied

Bysidian, "but this one won't give us any more trouble."

"I hope not, he was almost impossible to catch the first time around."

"Exactly how did you catch him Minister?" asked Bysidian curiously.

"He didn't tell you?"

"No, he wouldn't say."

"Then maybe somethings are better kept a secret," said the High Minister with a glint in his eye.

Outside the Granite Vault, three tiny pairs of ears were listening, fingers, toes and everything possible crossed the High Minister would not discover their deception.

The High Minister handed the black swirling pearl to Bysidian.

"Hide it well deep inside your vault Bysidian, make sure that creature is never found again."

Bysidian nodded and vanished into the cold and shadows of the eerie Night Warriors vault.

Higher and higher he climbed into the darkness way above the vault floor away from prying eyes and curious hands. The cold air froze his fingers as he placed the black pearl on a dusty ledge all alone.

Hurrying back across the Granite vault hoping for a quick escape Bysidian gave a respectful nod as he passed the waiting High Minister.

He knew the others were outside, listening and he did not want any more questions, the doorway was open, and he placed one foot outside. Freedom was within his reach.

"Wait," called the High Minister. Bysidian stopped and glanced at the three faces staring at him in horror hidden outside the door. Bysidian turned.

"May I ask how *you* caught him, the others did not say?"

"You may High Minister but as a wise man once said maybe some things are better kept a secret."

Watch out for these other titles

I hope you enjoyed The Goosebump Goblin. If you have a moment to spare, please do leave a review on Amazon. Your help with spreading the world of the Dream Drifters would be greatly appreciated.

Imagination can take you anywhere

dianebanhamimagine@outlook.com

Facebook @DianeBanhamAuthor

Instagram @dianebanham

Printed in Great Britain
by Amazon